LEGO

LEGENDS OF CHIMA™

D1392486

CLASH OF THE TRIBES

"Small Packages", "A Simple Bet", "The Hollow Tree", "The Challenge of Worriz" and "Lone Wolf … But Not By Choice" written by Greg Farshtey

LEGO, the LEGO logo, the Brick and Knob configurations, the Minifigure and LEGENDS OF CHIMA are trademarks of the LEGO Group. ©2013 The LEGO Group.

Produced by AMEET Sp. z o.o. under license from the LEGO Group.

AMEET Sp. z o.o.,
Przybyszewskiego 176/178, 93-120 Łódź – Poland
ameet@ameet.com.pl
www.ameet.pl

Penguin Books Ltd, 80 Strand, London, WC2R 0RL, UK
Please keep the Penguin Books Ltd address for future reference.

www.LEGO.com

ISBN: 9780723271192
001 - 10 9 8 7 6 5 4 3 2 1
Printed in Poland

Item name: LEGO® Legends of Chima™. Clash of the Tribes
Series: LNR
Item number: LNR 201/LNR 202
Batch: 01/GB

Ladybird

Published by Ladybird Books Ltd 2013
A Penguin Company
Penguin Books Ltd, 80 Strand, London, WC2R 0RL, UK
Penguin Books Australia Ltd, 707 Collins Street, Melbourne, Victoria 3008, Australia (a division of Pearson Australia Group Pty Ltd)

All rights reserved. No part of this publication may be reproduced, stored in a retrieval system, or transmitted in any form or by any means, electronic, mechanical, photocopying, recording or otherwise, without the prior consent of the copyright owner.

www.ladybird.com

CONTENTS

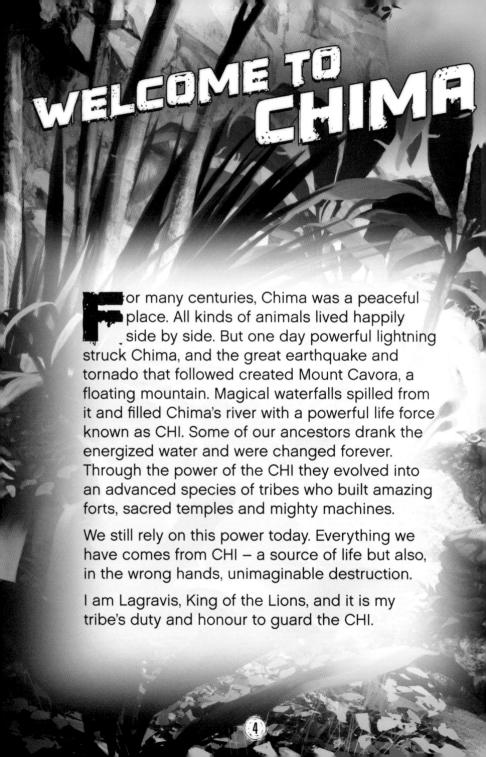

WELCOME TO CHIMA

For many centuries, Chima was a peaceful place. All kinds of animals lived happily side by side. But one day powerful lightning struck Chima, and the great earthquake and tornado that followed created Mount Cavora, a floating mountain. Magical waterfalls spilled from it and filled Chima's river with a powerful life force known as CHI. Some of our ancestors drank the energized water and were changed forever. Through the power of the CHI they evolved into an advanced species of tribes who built amazing forts, sacred temples and mighty machines.

We still rely on this power today. Everything we have comes from CHI – a source of life but also, in the wrong hands, unimaginable destruction.

I am Lagravis, King of the Lions, and it is my tribe's duty and honour to guard the CHI.

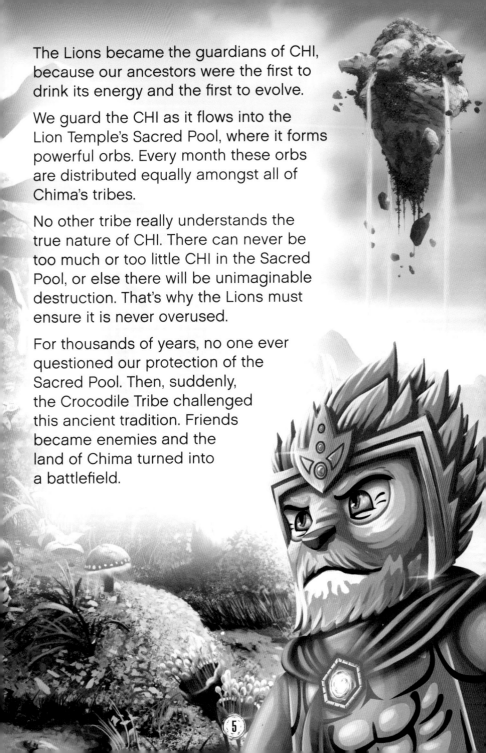

The Lions became the guardians of CHI, because our ancestors were the first to drink its energy and the first to evolve.

We guard the CHI as it flows into the Lion Temple's Sacred Pool, where it forms powerful orbs. Every month these orbs are distributed equally amongst all of Chima's tribes.

No other tribe really understands the true nature of CHI. There can never be too much or too little CHI in the Sacred Pool, or else there will be unimaginable destruction. That's why the Lions must ensure it is never overused.

For thousands of years, no one ever questioned our protection of the Sacred Pool. Then, suddenly, the Crocodile Tribe challenged this ancient tradition. Friends became enemies and the land of Chima turned into a battlefield.

SMALL PACKAGES

There are many things in this world that can be measured – the length of a day, the number of lions in a pride, the distance from one end of a valley to the other. And then there are those things that cannot be measured, no matter how hard one tries ... the courage in an animal's heart, the cleverness of his brain, the daring of his spirit. Only through experience can one learn the true amount of each of these in any living creature. – King Lagravis

"Muskrats?" Laval exclaimed in surprise. "Moles? Hedgehogs?!"

"Yes," said Lagravis, King of the Lions, to his son. "And beavers, rabbits and mice."

Laval shook his head in disgust. "You have to be joking!"

"I'm the king," Lagravis reminded him. "Kings do not joke. Very rarely we may laugh, but only very rarely."

"The Crocodiles and their allies attacked us!" Laval said angrily. "They want control of the CHI. We need powerful friends that can help us in this fight and you're suggesting moles and mice?"

"All of the animals have their role to play," Lagravis replied. "They may not all be as strong as the Gorilla or soar as high as the Eagle, but that does not mean they have no worth."

"To me, it does," Laval shot back. "What matters now are strength and speed and power. That's all the Crocs understand, and that's what we need in allies."

Later that day, Laval was still thinking about his talk with his father. He respected Lagravis more than anyone in the world, but sometimes his thinking was a little . . . old-fashioned. It was great to think everyone had the same value, big or small, but in a fight, he would vote for 'big' friends every time.

He climbed aboard his Speedor and raced off into the jungle. Driving fast always made it easier for him to think. He was sure the Crocodiles were planning some new raid, but where and when it might happen remained a mystery. He would just have to be ready for anything, he decided.

Suddenly, the mystery was solved: four Crocodiles on Speedorz™ roared out at him from both sides, trying to box him in. Laval shot his vehicle forward and avoided the trap, but now he had all four hot on his tail.

Using every trick he had learnt in his years of Speedor racing, Laval managed to stay ahead of his pursuers.

But he couldn't lose them. Worse still, they seemed to be trying to force him to go in certain directions, as if they were pushing him somewhere. Laval wondered if he was driving into another ambush up ahead.

As it turned out, there were no Crocodiles waiting along the path. What Laval ended up facing was far worse: the border of the desert. Stretching as far as the eye could see, there was nothing but sand and rocks, with no green growing anywhere.

This is very bad, thought Laval. If he turned back, he would have to fight the four Crocs. If he kept going forward, his Speedor – which depended on the presence of plants and trees for its power – would stop working. He would be stranded.

Laval was always sure he could win any fights, but four against one was enough to make him think twice.

The vehicle managed to make it only a short distance before the engine coughed and died. The Crocodiles didn't follow, not wanting their Speedorz to meet the same fate. They simply stood at the jungle's edge and watched.

Laval got off his Speedor. His best bet was to try to slip past the Crocs in a little while, when they started to get bored. If they got hungry, they might even head back to

the swamp. In the meantime, he needed to find shade and water, for there didn't seem to be any around.

The Lion Prince started walking south, always keeping one eye on the Crocodiles. After a while, he started to get tired and very thirsty. He was about to sit down and

take a rest when heard a very small voice from below say, "Hey, watch where you're sitting!"

Laval stopped and looked down. There was a little desert mouse waving a tiny fist at him. "You big guys think you can do whatever you want!" said the mouse. "Well, this is my property, right here, not yours."

"*This* is your property? Where?" asked Laval, smiling.

"From that pebble over there," the mouse said, pointing to the north. Then he pointed south. "Then all the way to that sand dune down there."

"Well, I'm sorry, I didn't know I was trespassing," said Laval.

"It's OK," said the mouse. "Hey, you're a long way from home, aren't you? There aren't any Lions in the desert."

Laval explained why he was there. "I won't be staying any longer than I have to, but I better find water pretty soon."

"Stick with me," the mouse said, with a smile. "I know all the best places. My name is Alonz, by the way."

Alonz scampered off, with Laval following. After a few minutes, they came to a very small oasis. Laval knelt down and drank. The water was salty, but still tasted good.

"Thanks," said Laval. "Now maybe I can sneak past the Crocs and get back home."

"That might be hard," said Alonz, pointing past Laval. The Lion turned to see that the four Crocs had advanced into the desert and were heading in his direction, though they hadn't spotted him yet.

"You better find a place to hide," said Laval. "There's going to be a fight, and I don't want you to get hurt, little guy. You're too small to stand up to Crocs."

"Ha!" said Alonz. "You don't have to be big to win a fight... and sometimes you don't even need to fight to win. Those Crocodiles are in my territory now. I'll show you how to handle them!"

The mouse raced off towards the Crocodiles. "Wait!" shouted Laval. "I'm coming with you!"

"You'll just get in the way," the mouse yelled back, cheerfully.

"Wait a minute!" Laval said, using a paw to block the mouse's path. "You can't take on four Crocs by yourself! You're just a mouse!"

"This is my home," Alonz replied. "I'm going to defend it. Besides, did you ever stop to think that maybe around here, you're 'just' a Lion?"

While Laval was thinking about that, the mouse scampered away. When he was about 10 feet from the Crocodiles, Alonz started jumping up and down and waving his arms. "Hey, Crocs!" yelled the mouse. "What's big and dumb and smells of swamp? You guys!"

One of the Crocodiles glanced at another. "It's a mouse."

"Yeah," said the other Croc.

"Should I step on him?"

"Nah, just let him squeak. It's good for a laugh."

But the Crocs weren't laughing for long, as Alonz ran around them, insulting their looks, their intelligence and their body odour. After a while, the Crocs started to get angry at the little mouse. They started to run after him, and Alonz took off as fast as his little legs could carry him. The Crocs were able to cover much more ground with each step and were catching up quickly. Laval was about to spring out to help his new friend when the four Crocs suddenly sank into the sand up to their waists.

Alonz stopped running, turned round, and laughed. "See, Laval? I told you. They might be bigger and stronger, but they don't know the desert. I do, especially where the patches of sinking sand are."

Laval walked up to the four Crocs. "Looks like you've been beaten ... by a mouse. What do you think Cragger will say?"

All four Crocs gulped hard.

"So this is what's going to happen," Laval continued. "I'll help you out of that sand before you sink up to your snouts, and you'll go back to the swamp. In return, I won't tell your king about what happened here today. Deal?"

The Crocs grumbled a lot, but agreed.

Later, after they had left, Laval dragged his Speedor back to the edge of the jungle, with Alonz perched on the seat. As soon as they were near the trees and plants, the engine roared to life. Startled, Alonz jumped on to Laval's shoulder.

"Why don't you come home with me?" asked the Lion. "I have to go and say I'm sorry to my dad. He was right about something, and I didn't see it until just now. I think he'd like to meet you."

"Will there be cheese?" asked Alonz.

"Probably," said Laval.

After a minute, Alonz said, "So what do you have to apologize for?"

"Oh, I had this idea that only small things come in small packages," answered Laval. "Turns out I was wrong."

LAVAL

"For the tribes – and for Chima! C'mon . . . It'll be fun!"

One day, Laval will take my place as the leader of our tribe. Before that can happen, the young prince has a lot to learn about rules and responsibility. Right now, he's more interested in adventure, fun and laughter. I believe in my son though, and know that he will grow to understand that sometimes you must sacrifice your own wishes for the greater good.

Laval is a great warrior. He is ruthless with sword and claw, he is master of the crushing lion pounce and, most of all, he is an undefeated Speedor racer.

Laval also hates greed and lies. He used to be best friends wtih Cragger, the Crocodile Prince. Unfortunately, Cragger changed into a scheming and aggressive rival and the two friends became sworn enemies. But Laval still hopes that the old friendship can one day be restored.

Lagravis' Challenge

As well as greed and lies, there are other things that Laval hates: water, too many rules, and people who can't take a joke. Which, do you think, worries me?

CHIMA FACTS

CHI transformed simple animals into advanced species, capable of inventing and building amazing things. It happened a thousand years ago, but the magical power of CHI has been used ever since.

Most inhabitants of Chima wear a special harness to hold a CHI orb. The CHI orb increases their strength, speed and stamina.

CHI is considered to be too powerful for children. Inhabitants of Chima have to reach the Age of Becoming before they are allowed to use it.

Every mechanical object in Chima has a special place where a CHI orb can be plugged in. The CHI orbs channel the magical power of nature into the engines of vehicles and all other machines. Even hand-held weapons are charged with CHI.

The most popular vehicles in Chima are one-wheeled Speedorz. Their wheels are carved from the rocks that fell from Mount Cavora. The wheels are part of nature and draw most energy from it. This is why the Speedorz are always the strongest in the lush jungles, but struggle to move in the deserts.

The power of the blue CHI orbs has its limits. In vehicles and machines the orbs can last up to several days, depending on how much power the mechanism requires. However, each month the Sacred Pool produces one Golden CHI orb that keeps its energy forever.

The Golden CHI is not simply given away. Each tribe sends a warrior to compete for it at the Grand Arena. The Golden CHI has the power to transform the arena and choose a different contest each month.

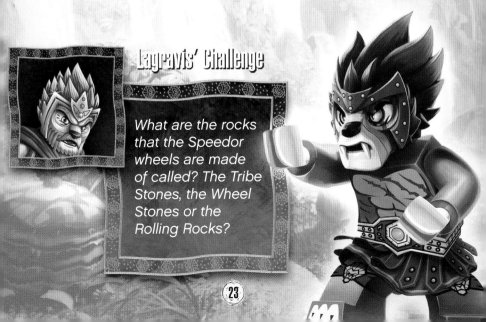

Lagravis' Challenge

What are the rocks that the Speedor wheels are made of called? The Tribe Stones, the Wheel Stones or the Rolling Rocks?

23

GREED FOR POWER

"No mercy. Ever.
Really. I mean it."

Cragger has always liked to compete, and loves to win. It was one of the things Laval liked about him when they first met. The two young princes soon became best friends, sharing a love for adventure, fun and the occasional prank. But everything changed when the two pranksters snuck into the Lion Temple to see the most hallowed place in the whole of Chima – the Sacred Pool of CHI. Despite Laval's desperate attempts to stop him, Cragger decided to break the rules and the Crocodile prince had his first taste of CHI. Cragger was too young to handle it and as a result he changed for the worse. Soon, Laval's best friend became his sworn enemy and the biggest threat to peace in Chima.

A SIMPLE BET

It was just about Cragger's favourite time of the day: lunchtime! He had asked the cooks to make him an especially good feast today, and he could already smell the wonderful food. Best of all, it was all for him – as King of the Crocodiles, he didn't have to share with anyone.

His sister, Crooler, saw him sitting at the table and came up to him. "Any food for me?" she asked.

"Nope," Cragger replied. "It's all mine."

"Right," his sister said, folding her arms. "Well, I can see it's not ready yet. Let's pass the time with a little bet."

"What kind of bet?" asked Cragger.

"Hmmmm," Crooler said. "I bet that you can't swim across the swamp and back in less than two minutes. If you win, you can have my next ration of CHI."

"I can do that easily," laughed Cragger, already thinking about how powerful some extra CHI would make him. He dived into the swamp and swam as fast as he could, making it to the far shore and back in record time.

"There!" he said. "I won!"

"Oh, wait, I forgot," said Crooler. "You have to do half the swim with your eyes closed."

Cragger was a little annoyed at this, but he knew he could still win the bet. So he swam across the swamp with his eyes closed, then back with his eyes open.

"OK, done. I won again," he said, starting to climb out of the swamp.

"Wait, wait," said Crooler. "I'm sorry, I made another mistake. You were supposed to dive all the way to the bottom halfway across, then do it again on the way back. And you have to keep your eyes closed the whole time."

Cragger glared at her. He knew his sister hated to lose bets, but this was getting ridiculous. "You can't keep changing the bet just because you lost," he snarled. "I won the CHI and it's mine."

"Just like how you will one day beat Laval and the Lions in battle and control the CHI. So don't tell me you're afraid of a little added difficulty in a simple bet."

"I'm not afraid of anything!" snapped Cragger. "I'll show you!"

And with that, he dived back into the swamp. Shutting his eyes, he started to swim through the muddy water.

When he judged he was about halfway across, he dived down. Now it didn't matter that his eyes were shut, because it was too dark down here to see anyway. He kept going until his nose struck the bottom, then he swam back up. Once he reached the surface, he made it to the far shore, turned round, and repeated what he had just done on his way back.

This time, he climbed all the way out of the water and stood on the shore. "Done. I won. You lost. Understand? I swam it under two minutes, and then I swam it with my eyes closed half the way, and then I did it with my eyes closed the whole way and dived to the swamp bottom on both legs of the trip. Now it's time for my lunch!"

Crooler shook her head sadly. "All right, all right. But I don't know how you think you can defeat Laval if you can't even beat your own sister in a bet."

"What are you talking about?" Cragger yelled. "I won the bet! W-O-N, won!"

"Well, if you call that winning," Crooler replied. "I mean, that was so easy that Crawley could have done it. You left out the part where you were supposed to count to five hundred when you were at the bottom."

Cragger felt like his head was going to explode. "I didn't leave that out, you left that out! You want me to count to

five hundred? Fine! But this is absolutely, positively, the last time I am doing this! When I win – and I will win – I want your CHI for the next two months, not just one."

Before Crooler could reply, Cragger turned and dived back into the swamp. He repeated the entire routine, including counting to five hundred both ways.

When he was done, he came ashore and opened his eyes. There was Crooler seated at the table, finishing off his lunch. As he watched, she popped the last morsel in her mouth and smacked her lips. "Mmmmm," she said. "I can see why you were looking forward to this so much!"

"Why, you – you..." sputtered Cragger.

"Oh, and by the way, you were supposed to do all that with one arm tied behind your back," Crooler said, smiling, "so you better get busy. I'm going to go take a nap. A good meal always makes me sleepy!"

Cragger was so angry he could barely speak. Now he would have to wait for the cooks to make *another* meal.

"Stupid bet," Cragger grumbled, sitting down on the shore.

Grumble, his empty stomach replied.

THE CROCODILE TRIBE

The Crocodiles have always been a sneaky, slippery bunch. They are tough fighters, and you can never completely trust them. However, under the rule of King Crominus, they followed the code of Chima and lived in harmony with the other tribes. But when the Crocodiles suddenly lost their king and queen, the young, ambitious Prince Cragger took the throne.

Encouraged by his twin sister, Crooler, the new king decided to try to take all of the CHI away from the Lions. He trusts his sister too much to realize that he is only a puppet in her game. Crooler may not be a strong or skilled warrior, but she is brilliant at manipulating others. She uses Cragger to achieve her own goals, while making fun of him behind his back. Under Crooler's bad influence, Cragger has become the fiercest of all Crocodiles, and even his own tribe members fear him.

The Crocodiles are on the same side as the Wolves and the Ravens. Equipped with powerful weapons and deadly battle machines, the three armies attacked the Lion Temple. Fortunately, with the help of our friends, the Eagles and the Gorillas, we managed to hold them off. But Cragger hates losing, so we are expecting a new attack at any time . . .

*"I'm not mean.
You're just weak."*

There are both good and bad sides to possessing great magical power. Those who do must understand the true nature of the CHI and use it responsibly.

Some of Chima's original inhabitants – the four-legged animals – did not drink from the CHI-energized waters. According to legend, they feared that evolution might change their world too, but for the worse.

These four-legged animals chose to stay 'pure'. Instead of drinking the magical water, they headed off into the Chima Outlands. No one ever saw them again. We call them the Legend Beasts, but not everyone believes they exist.

The water that flows through Chima no longer transforms the local creatures. However, the glowing orbs of CHI produced in the Sacred Pool are still used as a source of power by all the modern inhabitants of Chima.

Every tribe receives a monthly share of about fify CHI orbs. This amount has to energize their machinery, vehicles and the tribe members themselves for a whole month. So the orbs are used sparingly...unless there is a battle.

The orbs can be stored for a limited amount of time and used when needed. Warriors often carry an 'emergency' orb with them, but they utilize its power only when absolutely necessary.

Led by the young, but feared, Cragger, the ferocious Crocodile Tribe will stop at nothing until they take control of the CHI. The Crocodiles are skilful fighters who don't understand the meaning of the word 'mercy' – so it is pointless asking them for it.

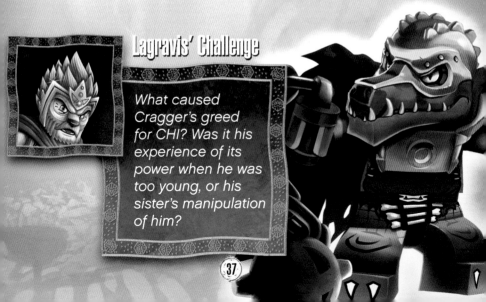

Lagravis' Challenge

What caused Cragger's greed for CHI? Was it his experience of its power when he was too young, or his sister's manipulation of him?

CHIMA QUIZ

How much have you learnt about the land of Chima and its inhabitants? Test your knowledge with this quiz, then turn the page to check your answers.

1. What created the floating mountain, Mount Cavora?
a) A terrible flood
b) Powerful lightning
c) A volcanic eruption

2. What happened to the animals that drank the magical water?
a) They grew an extra pair of legs and wings
b) They disappeared for a thousand years
c) They evolved into smarter, two-legged animals

3. Which animal species first drank the energized water?
a) The Wolves
b) The Crocodiles
c) The Lions

4. Where do the CHI orbs form?
a) In the Sacred Pool inside the Lion Temple
b) In the Sacred Pool on top of Mount Cavora
c) In the Sacred Pool hidden in Chima swamps

5. **What effect does CHI have on those who take it?**
   a) It enables them to float in the air
   b) It makes them glow in the dark
   c) It gives them incredible power

6. **Who was too young to try CHI, but did it anyway?**
   a) Laval
   b) Cragger
   c) Crooler

7. **What is Laval, the Lion Prince, especially good at?**
   a) Following the rules
   b) Speedor racing
   c) Crushing apple pies

8. **How can a tribe get a super-powerful orb of Golden CHI?**
   a) They have to win it in a contest
   b) They can buy it or exchange goods for it
   c) They have to wait until it falls off Mount Cavora

9. **What is Crooler's extraordinary talent?**
   a) The ability to operate complex machines
   b) The ability to manipulate her brother
   c) The ability to befriend everyone

10. **Who took the side of the Crocodiles against the Lions?**
   a) The Eagle Tribe
   b) The Wolf Tribe
   c) The Gorilla Tribe

BATTLE FOR CHI

I am Lagravis, King of the Lion Tribe, who guard Chima's greatest treasure – the CHI.

Thousands of years ago, Chima was an unspoiled land, filled with lush jungles and simple, four-legged animals. One day, lightning struck Chima and tore Mount Cavora out of the ground. Magical waterfalls spilled from the floating mountain, filling the river on the ground below with a mysterious life force. Some animals drank the energized water and transformed into two-legged creatures. The incredible energy empowered our ancestors to develop advanced technology and build amazing structures. Today, CHI powers everything we have created. It can also enhance our strength, abilities and instincts, if used wisely. My tribe shared the orbs of CHI fairly with each tribe. But later with the help of the Wolves and the Ravens, the Crocodiles tried to take all the CHI for themselves, causing a fierce battle between us.

Luckily, we have allies too …

ERIS

The are other Eagles like her, but many of them think that Eris is very eccentric. She isn't particularly strong, but she is very intelligent and believes you can win battles by talking and using clever tactics, rather than fighting. Eris is a very reliable friend and is always willing to help everyone out. Just don't let her corner you and tell you her jokes – most of them aren't as funny as she thinks they are!

Lagravis' Challenge

Eris supports the Lion Tribe in the conflict over the CHI, because she hates Cragger, the Crocodile Tribe's leader. True or false?

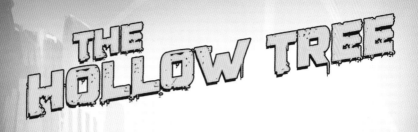

THE HOLLOW TREE

Eris flew over the tree-tops, wondering how things could have become so bad so fast. First, the Crocodiles had insisted they get more of their share of CHI and attacked the Lions. Then they enlisted the Wolves as allies. *The Crocs have to be crazy to trust Wolves*, she thought, *but together they make a very dangerous pack.*

The Wolves had already caused all sorts of problems. They had driven the groundhogs away from their favourite watering hole, torn up the rabbit dens with their trucks, and generally had everyone in the area afraid and wishing the pack would leave.

But the Wolves weren't hanging around just to cause trouble. Ewald, the leader of the Eagles' Ruling Council, had told her that the pack was hiding in the woods somewhere near by, waiting for a chance to ambush the Lions on their way to distribute CHI. But no one knew where in the woods the Wolves were. Someone had to find out where they were hiding so the Lions could be warned.

Now how am I supposed to find a bunch of Wolves? Eris said to herself. *Let's see, I could disguise myself as a chicken... no, that would never work. I'm too big, chicken feathers make me itch, and I'm way cuter than any chicken could be. I need a better plan.*

She soared over an open field that bordered the forest. Down below, a lone tree stood out amidst the grass. Eris landed on a high branch and thought hard.

The Wolves might be just past the edge of the woods, watching me right now, she said to herself. *But how do I make them show themselves? Hmmmm... Wolves like to eat... and howl at the moon... and make fun of other animals, but they don't like it when anyone makes fun of them.*

Eris smiled. That was it. No one was as quick-witted as she was. She would tease the Wolves until they got so angry they would forget they were supposed to be hiding!

She looked down at the tree. It was hollow, and squirrels used it to hide their nuts in the winter. Maybe she could use it as part of her plan.

Eris flew inside the tree through a hole in the trunk. Then she turned and thrust her head back through the hole, yelling, "Hey! Why did the Wolves cross the road? They were running away from the Lions!"

As soon as she said it, she ducked back into the tree. After a few moments, she poked her head back out again. "How many Wolves does it take to get an apple off a tree? Ninety-seven... one to hold the apple and ninety-six to lift up the tree."

This time, Eris thought she heard a couple of growls from the woods as she dived back into the tree. When she stuck her head out of the hole, she yelled extra loud, "Stop me if you've heard this one: Knock, knock. Who's there? Worriz. Worriz who?"

Eris waited a moment, then laughed, "Worriz the best place to hide? These woods are scary!"

Then she could hear angry grumbling coming from the forest. She puffed out her chest and made her voice as rough as could be, saying, "Look at me! I'm a Wolf. I'm the toughest animal in the forest and every other animal is afraid of me … well, the mice are … and the ants … and maybe some frogs. If I see a hedgehog,

I run away – but I look really tough while I'm doing it!"

That last joke did it. The Wolves came surging out of the oak trees, growling and snapping their jaws, as they charged towards the hollow tree. Before Eris could get out of the hole and take flight, they were all around her hiding place.

Uh-oh, thought Eris. *Now what?*

She looked all around for something that would help her escape the Wolves. Then she saw some piles of nuts that the squirrels had left and she scooped them up and threw them at the Wolves, tripping them up. Every time the Wolves tried to get up, they kept slipping on the nuts!

Whilst the Wolves were distracted. Eris flew out of the hole in the tree and up into the sky. She raced back to tell Ewald that the wolves were near the oak trees and to let the Lions know.

And all because, Eris thought with a smile, *my jokes drove them nuts!*

THE WINGED ALLIES

The Eagle Tribe lives on Chima's mysterious rock spires. Living high above the clouds gives the Eagles a unique outlook on the world. They are observers and thinkers, wise but also a little bit spacey. If you let them start talking, you may have to listen to their philosophical theories for hours on end. But they are great fighters too, and any enemy who dares to threaten them should beware of their fierce aerial assaults.

When Cragger, the Crocodile King, led his army to attack the Lion Temple, I had no choice but to call on friends to help us. The Eagles were the first to arrive on the battlefield. They knew that we, the Lions, have been guarding the CHI to keep the natural balance of Chima, and we have always shared it equally with other tribes — even with those we weren't friendly with. Supported by our winged allies, we can keep up the ancient order and protect our world from untold calamities that may happen when all the CHI falls into Cragger's greedy claws.

EVEN MORE CHIMA FACTS

All Chima tribes rely on CHI. Its incredible energy enables us to build complicated machinery that makes our lives more comfortable. But now that the conflict over the CHI rages on, our inventions are often used for battle . . .

Lagravis' Challenge
The first Speedor wheels – the CHI-energized hearts of the Speedorz used by all tribes in Chima – were parts of Mount Cavora. True or false?

The Eagle Tribe is the most advanced of all Chima tribes, intellectually as well as in science and technology. All animals construct machines and design them in their own image. The Eagles take pride in design, efficiency and aerodynamics.

Despite their natural abilities, the Eagles build flying machines too. They even modify their Speedorz – Chima's most popular ground driven vehicles – just by adding two CHI-powered propellers at the sides to make them fly.

The Eagles' craftsmanship is challenged by no one. They use only the most exquisite of metals to build their elegant machines. The claws of the Eagle planes (that also act as a landing gear) are made from the finest most hardened metal and the force of their grip is awesome.

Any dent, scratch or malfunction of the Eagle machines caused by use or battle is immediately repaired in maintenance hangars. The Eagles would never take off in a less than fully operational, sharp-looking and immaculately clean plane.

Out of all the Chima tribes, only the Eagle engineers have mastered the ability to use the CHI power in almost silent jet-like technology. This makes them the fastest of the airborne species of Chima. When reaching top speed, the jets emit a piercing high-pitched eagle shriek.

Worriz is the Wolf tribe's lead negotiator, and the closest thing the wild Wolves have to a 'responsible leader'. He is a vicious and ruthless creature who loves a well-executed betrayal, but is able to disguise his true nature to fool others.

He can even occasionally fake a bit of charm when needed. When he was younger, he hung around with all species. But that was because, as the adult Worriz claims, he didn't know any better. Worriz thinks the alliance with the Crocodiles against the Lions will be profitable for the Wolves, so his current 'best friend' is Cragger. Worriz seeks personal revenge against my son, Laval, for a Speedor joust that ended badly for the wolf. He also wants to rule the whole of Chima, should Cragger ever fall – or be pushed – from power.

Eris perched on a rock and gazed down at the ground far below, frowning. Just as she had for the last six days, she could see Wolves prowling at the base of the cliffs that the Eagles called home. Now and then, one would look up at her, flash a savage grin, and howl. She did her best to ignore the taunts.

Ever since the Crocodiles and Lions had clashed over the sharing of CHI among the tribes, the Wolves had been encroaching on Eagle territory. Normally, Wolves were constantly on the move, but this pack was acting like they were here to stay. They were noisy, messy, and threw loud parties late into the night so that none of the eagles could sleep.

It would all have been just a bit inconvenient if it wasn't for two things: one, the Eagles needed to be able to fly down to the ground to find food, and the Wolves were making that dangerous to do. And two, it was almost time for the Eagles to get their share of the powerful CHI from the Lions, and Eris was sure the Wolves were here to prevent that from happening.

If only we could find some way to make them go away, she thought. *But how?*

Just then, Eglor – the Eagle Tribe's inventor and engineer – flew by, shouting, "I've done it! I've done it!" The Wolves looked up to see what the commotion was all about.

"Shhhh!" said Eris. "What have you done?"

But Eglor was too excited to speak quietly. "I've perfected a machine that can hurl an Eagle all the way from one end of the forest to the other, faster than any beast who can run or fly! From now on, instead of flap, flap, flap to get from one place to another, it will be zip, zip, zip!"

"Zip, zip, zip?" said one of the Wolves, laughing. "Sounds more like flop, flop, flop to me!"

Eglor wheeled in the air and looked down at the Wolf. "Ha! With my machine, any Eagle could outrace any Wolf. That's just scientific fact. There's not even the teeniest, tiniest, most microscopic speck of doubt."

"Want a bet?" growled Worriz. The pack leader had wandered over to see what the rest of the Wolves were so interested in. Then he eyed Eglor and smiled mockingly.

"Arguing with Wolves doesn't do any good."

But Eglor's pride as an inventor was now at stake. "Yes, I do!" he said loudly.

"All right, then," said Worriz. "I bet you I can make it to the far end of the woods faster than any Eagle launched from your machine.

If I win, you Eagles give up your share of CHI to us this month."

"And if you lose," said Eglor, "you go away and leave our nesting area alone!"

Eris slapped a wing against her forehead. What had Eglor just gotten them into?

"Deal," said Worriz. "We race tomorrow ... that is, if you can find someone foolish enough to challenge me."

"Tomorrow?" said Eglor. "Now, see here, the machine works ... I know it does ... but it hasn't been tested yet, and ..."

The Wolves howled with laughter. One of them said, "You know what they say about Eagles – all flash and feathers."

"If you want to back down, bird ..." Worriz sneered.

"I'll do it!" said Eris. "I'll race you!"

After she had said it, she could hardly believe the words had come out of her beak. But the Wolves were getting under her feathers with all their insults and maybe this was the one way to get them to leave the neighbourhood. Besides, Eglor was a great inventor – if he said his machine could make her go zip, zip, zip, then it could.

"One more rule," snapped Worriz. "No help from Lions, right, Eagle?"

All the Wolves laughed.

* * *

"It can't," said Eglor, sadly.

"What do you mean?" asked Eris, in shock. "You said it worked!"

It was the middle of the night. Eglor had taken Eris to see his machine, which consisted of a long piece

of metal with a bowl at the end, attached to a much bigger metal apparatus by tightly wound springs. When Eglor triggered the contraption, the bowl would be propelled forward and anything inside it would go flying . . . at least, in theory.

"I tested it this afternoon, and it worked fine," Eglor explained. "But then I started practising tonight with things actually in the bowl, like apples, and . . . well, look for yourself."

Eris looked. There were mashed apples all over the floor of Eglor's workshop. The machine just hurled them straight down at the ground.

"So if I get in this thing tomorrow morning ... no zip?" she said.

"More like squish," said Eglor. "We'll have to call off the bet."

"We can't," insisted Eris. "The Wolves will tell the Crocodiles and make us look weak ... we'll lose our CHI ... and the Wolves will stay down there forever! I have to win the race ... somehow. I just have to."

* * *

"Did you do it?" whispered Worriz.

Wilhurt nodded. "It was easy. I used a bellow plant to float up the mountain and then tied it down. I got to Eglor's workshop, and broke part of his machine. Then, I let the air out of the bellow plant little by little so I could float back down. That Eagle won't be zipping anywhere, boss."

"Good," Worriz said with a wolfish grin. "All that Eagle CHI is practically ours. Hey, maybe we'll challenge the Bears and the Gorillas to races, too. Let the Crocodiles fight battles — we'll get all the CHI we want the old-fashioned way: we'll cheat."

* * *

By dawn, Eris had a plan . . . sort of. It started with not telling Worriz the machine didn't work. The second part involved getting some help from someone she would normally stay far away from.

Skinnet was actually a very nice animal, who didn't have an enemy in the world. But no one really wanted to spend any time around him because, sometimes he smelled really bad. It wasn't his fault, he was a skunk, but no one wanted to risk keeping him company and

maybe ending up smelling terrible too. Still, Eris had always made an effort to be polite to him.

"Skinnet, can you do me a favour?" she asked, talking to him from high up in a tree.

"Me? Really? You want me to do you a favour?" Skinnet said eagerly. No one ever asked him to do anything other than go away.

"That's right," said Eris. "It's nothing hard. I just want you to do . . . that thing you do at a certain place and a certain time."

Skinnet frowned. Making a stink always made other animals run away. Why would Eris want him to do that?

"Just trust me," Eris reassured him. "You'll be doing something nice for all the eagles."

"If you say so," Skinnet answered, smiling. "But better hold your beak — it's going to get smelly around here!"

* * *

After making a few more stops, Eris was ready for the start of the race. She perched in Eglor's lab, waiting for the signal to start. Down below, Worriz was crouched down, ready to run.

One of the wolves waved a palm leaf and the race began. Eris flew as fast as she could. Anyone looking

from below would think she had been rocketed into the sky. Worriz was running at top speed too, hoping to put some distance between himself and the Eagle.

As she soared above the canopy of trees, Eris did her best to keep an eye on Worriz, even if she could only see him for a few seconds now and then. She knew the wolf would take the fastest path through the forest. In fact, she was counting on it.

In the woods, Worriz was feeling confident. The pack had blazed a new trail through the forest lately, one that made getting from one end to the other a breeze. All he had to do was follow the scent the vehicles had left and he couldn't go wrong. He put his nose to the ground, took a big sniff... and almost fell over!

His nose was full of an incredibly horrible smell, so bad it made his eyes water. He shook his head violently, trying to make the odour go away, but it didn't. It was so overpowering that now he couldn't smell anything else. Worriz knew there was only one animal in the forest who could make a smell that bad.

"Skinnet!" he yelled.

Off to the side of the path, the little skunk ran away, disappearing into the foliage.

All right, I don't need my nose, Worriz grumbled to himself. *I can remember the path… sort of. I know there were trees… and a big rock… and some dirt… hmmm…*

Worriz picked a direction that looked right and started running again. At one point, he glanced up and spotted Eris through the trees. She was falling behind. All he had to do was put on an extra burst of speed and he was sure to win.

He heard an enormous rustling in the wood just ahead. It sounded like a huge herd of creatures on the move, but there was no pounding of feet to accompany it. As he rounded a bend, he discovered why: it was a tribe of Gorillas in their massive Gorilla Mechs, being extra careful not to disturb anything as they passed.

This courtesy towards nature meant that the Gorillas had to move very slowly in their huge machines, so as to make sure they did not accidentally trample any flowers or even weeds.

"Come on!" Worriz growled. "Hurry it up!"

Three of the gorillas stopped dead right in Worriz's path. "Hey, Wolf, why are you in such a hurry?" said the first Gorilla, looking down from the cockpit of his mech.

"Yeah, you have to savour every minute of life, the way you do a really good banana," said the second.

"Maybe you just don't see it," said the third. "You Wolves always have your noses to the ground and you don't ever look up."

The Gorillas proceeded to tell Worriz all about how much better life was when you were in tune with nature. All the other Gorillas stopped to listen, nodding their heads and smiling. It felt like forever before they finally finished and moved on, the mechs moving even more slowly than before.

When the gorillas had passed, Worriz ran faster than he ever had. He was heading for the fast-moving river that

ran through this part of the forest. If he dived in and let the waters carry him, he could still beat Eris. OK, it was against the rules, but so what? The only thing that mattered to him was winning.

He was just about to the riverbank when a group of small figures appeared in his path. They were young foxes, at least two dozen of them, all smiling and yipping and jumping up and down.

"Look, it's Worriz!"

"I told you he was coming!"

"Wow, look how cool he looks!"

"I have to get his pawprint! I just have to!"

Before Worriz knew what was happening, he was being mobbed by the foxes. They were tugging at his fur and running back and forth in front of him.

"We're your biggest fans," said one of the foxes breathlessly. "We listen to all your howls!"

"Could you howl for us now? Please, please, please!" said another.

"Get out of my way!" roared Worriz.

But the foxes wouldn't move. Worriz had to elbow his way past them and, even then, they wouldn't stop chasing after him. They followed him all the way to the edge of the woods, only leaving when he arrived the plain to see Eris waiting for him.

"I won," said the Eagle. "So pack up your pack and move on."

"Ha!" said Worriz. "Your Lion pals aren't here, so you can't prove you won the race."

Eris pointed up the sky. A whole flock of sparrows was circling overhead, all cheering wildly for Eris.

"Don't you know it by now?" the eagle said, smiling. "I have *lots* of friends."

THE WOLF TRIBE

The Wolves live in Woodlands, but they are a travelling tribe and they never stay in one place very long. Their convoys are made up of rough-looking battle vehicles that resemble military assault squads. They sleep in tightly-packed piles so they can cram an unusual amount of warriors into their mobile homes.

Everyone in the pack is somebody's brother, sister or cousin, and they will do anything for each other. Group decisions are usually arrived at easily and unanimously, so there is no real need for leaders. However, the Wolves' transitory nature and travelling battle-caravans often bring them into contact (and conflict) with other creatures' mobile homes. Because of this someone in the tribe has to handle negotiations with 'the others' (as all non-Wolves are known). Worriz was given this role because he was considered 'the most personable'.

The Wolves are ferocious fighters, but they have no problem running away from a battle they don't think they can win. They are not driven by emotions, but calculate the risk involved in their actions. For them it's not about pride or glory, it's all about getting the job done with minimum sacrifice. Win, lose, cheat, run away ... all they want is for the pack to survive and thrive.

YET MORE CHIMA FACTS

The Wolves' vehicles have everything that keeps them going in all terrains: big tyres, flexible suspension and powerful engines. The machines are as ferocious as their owners!

Lagravis' Challenge
The Wolves are extremely jealous of the Eagles' ability to build their awesome, shiny and elegant machines. True or false?

The sharp edges give the Wolf Tribe's machines a fierce, predatory look. Their design screams 'DO NOT TOUCH! You will get hurt', but the sharpness has a practical purpose too – the vehicles can easily cut their way through dense forest.

The Wolves put their vehicles together with a large number of rivets and decorate them with skins, teeth and chains. Usually painted grey, the vehicles blend perfectly into most environments. It's often very hard to tell where a Wolf convoy ends and the woods begin.

The Wolves are efficient and ram breakable objects instead of going round them. This leaves their thick metal-plated vehicles dented and scratched. But as they are very well constructed and durable, it does not effect their performance or efficiency, so the Wolves see no reason to repair them.

In the engines an extreme heat combustion process burns the CHI to release its energy. As a result, a loud roaring is heard and bright flames shoot from exhaust pipes. The Wolves sneak in close and then rev their engines up and howl wildly as part of their scare and confuse tactics when they attack.

The Wolves have CHI-powered pulse cannons fitted on to their vehicles from which they fire a quick series of short semi powerful bursts. Those weapons could be very useful in battle, but aiming is not easy when your vehicle is running at a crazy speed through the thick jungle!

LONE WOLF...
BUT NOT BY CHOICE

It was dinner time for the Wolf pack. That meant three things: meat, meat and more meat. Everyone gathered around and did their part to devour the day's feast. It was a special celebration tonight – the Wolves had come back from a huge raid on the Lion camp and stolen loads of food. All the Wolves were chomping and chewing and having a good time.

Everyone, that was, except Wonald.

For as far back as he could remember, Wonald had always been a ... different kind of Wolf. While his friends all howled at the moon, Wonald loved basking in the sunshine. While the other Wolves snarled and growled at anyone who came too near the pack, Wonald would try to make friends with them. But it was at dinner time that Wonald's different approach to Wolf life was most obvious.

"Wonald, what are you doing?" snarled Windra. She was a beautiful white wolf, but as fierce and dangerous as anyone else in the pack, and a great deal more so than some.

"Um, well, I'm, well ..." Wonald stammered. "I'm actually making a salad."

Windra looked down at the pile of lettuce, tomatoes and other vegetables Wonald had gathered on a big, flat tree stump. She took a sniff and then crinkled up her nose as if totally disgusted. "Hard as it might be to believe, Wonald, you are a Wolf. Wolves do not eat salad. Wolves eat meat."

"I don't like meat," Wonald explained.

Windra leaned in close. "It doesn't matter if you like it or not. You are a Wolf, and it's what we do!"

Wonald shrugged. "Well, it's not what I do. Besides, if I don't have any, then there's more for everyone else, right?"

Windra growled in frustration and stalked away.

As he always did, Wonald went off on his own to eat.

That way, he wouldn't provoke any jokes from the other Wolves, or have to watch them gulping down their dinners. After the meal was over, though, the Wolves did what they usually did: they got into a fight among themselves, growling and snapping and biting.

"Stop it!" Wonald said. "Why do we have to fight all the time, just because we're Wolves?"

The Wolves responded by snapping at him, until Wonald finally left and went off to bed.

When Wonald woke up the next morning, it was very quiet. That wasn't unusual – most Wolves tended to sleep late. He got up, stretched, and headed for camp to see if he had any berries left for his breakfast.

That was when he got a terrible shock.

There was no sign of the other Wolves anywhere. All the vehicles were gone too. It looked like the whole camp had been packed up overnight and taken somewhere else.

Now, it was true that the Wolves did this sort of thing all the time. They hated to stay in one place for very long. What made Wonald's heart sink down to his feet was that they had moved on without him. He had been left behind!

It must be my fault, he thought to himself. *They must have got tired of how 'different' I am and decided to kick me out of the pack. But I don't want to be on my own. I have to find them!*

Wonald sniffed the ground. Years of using his nose to tell which vegetables were good and which were rotten had left him with a great sense of smell. He could tell the pack had gone north west. Wonald started to follow them.

After a short time, he came to a fork in the path. The pack had gone right, the wheels of their vehicles tearing up the ground and wrecking a meerkat nest. The meerkats were busily trying to repair the damage. Wonald walked over and said, "Can I help?"

"Look at this mess!" snapped one of the meerkats. "We just finished cleaning up for the big family reunion – all fifteen thousand, one hundred and sixty-seven of our relatives are coming over – and some bunch of Wolves knocked down our house!"

"I'm sure they didn't mean it," said Wonald. "They were probably just in a hurry. Here, let me clear some of this dirt away from your holes for you."

When Wonald had finished helping the meerkats rebuild their nest, he set out on the Wolf trail again. It wasn't long before he came upon some young trees that had been knocked over. A bunch of squirrels were running to and fro, gathering nuts that were scattered on the ground.

"Nuts, nuts, nuts!" said one of the squirrels.

"Yes, there are certainly a lot of them," agreed Wonald.

"No, I mean, nuts to those Wolves who knocked down our trees!" said the squirrel. "We put all our nuts in these trees, and now they're all over the place. Of course, I wanted to put our nuts into the First Nut Bank of the

Forest, but oh no, my husband knows better. 'Put them in the trees,' he says, 'they'll be safer there.' Ha!"

Wonald began picking up nuts and bringing them over to the pile the squirrels were making. As soon as they noticed him, all the squirrels backed away.

"Go ahead!" said one squirrel. "Take the nuts! We can find more!"

"I don't want your nuts . . . though they do look tasty," said Wonald, who hadn't had his breakfast yet. "I'm just trying to help you clean up."

"Oh," said the squirrels. "Oh. Well, that's all right then. Keep going."

Once that job was finished, Wonald moved on. He couldn't believe how much damage the wolves were doing as they travelled. The scent was getting stronger though, so he knew he would soon catch up with them.

Wonald came to a rushing river. On the shore, a little beaver was crying. "What's the matter?" asked the Wolf.

"My beautiful dam!" said the beaver. "Some Wolves came by and broke it to pieces as they crossed the river. It will take me hours and hours to fix."

"It's OK," said Wonald. He knew from experience that beavers will talk all day long, if given the chance. "I'll give you a paw rebuilding your dam."

The Wolf and the beaver worked together to fix the broken dam. When they were finished, the beaver offered Wonald some tree bark as a snack. Wonald said no – he wasn't that hungry. Besides, he could hear the pack not far ahead, growling and snarling.

Wonald ran towards the sound. Up ahead, he could see Windra and the other Wolves chasing some rabbits away from their grazing ground. The passage of the pack had already torn a lot of the grass up from the ground.

"Hey! Stop!" Wonald called, rushing forward. "Leave the rabbits alone!"

"What are you going to do about it?" growled one of the Wolves, without turning round. "Get lost!"

"I already was lost," said Wonald. "I thought I was found again, but the way the pack has been wrecking everything they see today . . . well, maybe I was better off not knowing where you were."

The Wolf he was speaking to looked over his shoulder. His eyes widened a little and his jaw dropped. "It's Wonald! Hey, everybody, it's Wonald!" he howled.

"Wonald? Where?"

"Did someone say Wonald?"

"Out of the way, let me see!"

The whole pack suddenly surrounded the young wolf. Even the rabbits stopped running and watched the whole scene, puzzled. Wonald didn't know what it all meant either.

"You ran off and left me," said Wonald. "But now you seem so glad to see me. I don't understand."

"We didn't abandon you," said Windra. "You abandoned us. When it was time to move out, you were nowhere to be found."

"I didn't know you were leaving!" insisted Wonald.

"Worriz told us right after supper," said one of the Wolves. "Didn't you hear him?"

Wonald suddenly remembered that he had walked out after supper. He had missed the pack leader's speech to the other Wolves, so didn't know the pack was travelling on before dawn.

"We looked for you, but couldn't find you," said Windra.

"I came looking for you, but only saw all the damage you have been doing in the forest," said Wonald.

"Well, we were upset," said an older wolf. "We thought you had deserted the pack. You might not always act like we do, but you are still one of us, Wonald. And we missed you."

"All right, enough," snapped Windra. "He's back. So we better find a new place to camp for the night, preferably where there are plenty of . . ." She gave Wonald a long look, and then said, "Vegetables."

Wonald smiled.

That night, he had his usual salad for dinner. But this time, when the others went to howl at the moon, Wonald went with them. He still thought it was kind of a silly thing to do, but they were his friends after all.

Together, the Wolves howled happily until dawn.

CHIMA QUIZ

Now that you have learnt more about the new tribes of Chima, it is time to test your memory. Read the questions carefully and circle the right answer.

1. **Which tribe has allied with the Lions to protect the CHI?**
   a) The Wolves
   b) The Crocodiles
   c) The Eagles

2. **What makes Eris different from other Eagles?**
   a) She loves poetry and philosophy
   b) She is always focussed and quick-witted
   c) She prefers fighting to talking

3. **Who led the attack on the Lion Temple?**
   a) Cragger
   b) Lagravis
   c) Worriz

4. **Why has the Lion Tribe been guarding the CHI?**
   a) Because no other tribe really wanted to do it
   b) To keep the natural balance in Chima
   c) To have all the CHI for themselves

5. **Which Chima tribe is intellectually the most advanced of all?**
   a) The Lions
   b) The Crocodiles
   c) The Eagles

6. **What is the unique achievement of the Eagle engineers?**
   a) Almost silent jet-like technology powered by CHI
   b) Self-repairable flying battle machines
   c) Scratch-proof metal used for the most elegant planes

7. **What is so special about the Wolves?**
   a) They never stay long in one place
   b) They are Chima's best negotiators
   c) They sleep in the daytime and travel at night

8. **What is the Wolves' favourite combat strategy?**
   a) High-speed attack with high pitched shriek
   b) Sneak in close, scare and confuse
   c) Sneak in close, observe and run away

9. **What is the true nature of Worriz?**
   a) He is kind and reasonable
   b) He is charming but foolish
   c) He is vicious and ruthless

10. **Why does Worriz seek revenge against Laval?**
   a) Because Laval once stole his CHI
   b) Because Laval defeated him in a Speedor joust
   c) Bacause Laval damaged his Speedor badly

ANSWERS

Page 21
Laval

Young Prince Laval, the future king, has a relentless flair for challenging the rules. This can be a problem as the Lions are all about following and enforcing order.

Page 23
Chima Facts

When the first four-legged animals of each species drank from the CHI-energized waters and evolved into two-legged creatures, part of Mount Cavora crumbled away revealing giant carvings of those species' heads. The rocks that fell down from the mountain at that time were called Tribe Stones.

Page 37
More Chima Facts

Actually, both. Cragger has loved the power of CHI ever since he disregarded the rules and tried it. When Cragger became the King of the Crocodiles, Crooler convinced him that he should fight the Lions for control over the CHI. Enchanted by the smell of a strange magical flower that Crooler held under his nose, Cragger took this decision without hesitation.

Pages 38–39
Chima Quiz

1. – B; 2. – C; 3. – C; 4. – A; 5. – C;
6. – B; 7. – B; 8. – A; 9. – B; 10. – B.

Page 41
Eris

False. Eris just wants everyone to get along. She doesn't care who wins or loses, as long as everyone stops fighting and there is peace in the world. She will do whatever it takes to make that happen, even if it is not in her own best interests.

Page 49
Even More Chima Facts

True. When the first four-legged animal of each species drank the CHI-energized water and evolved, a part of Mount Cavora crumbled away to reveal a carving of the species' head. Altogether only eight carvings were created. The rocks that fell to the ground during the creation of these carvings are known as Tribe Stones. Our ancestors carved these Tribe Stones into Speedor Wheels of extraordinary strength and power.

Page 67
Yet More Chima Facts

False. The Wolves absolutely loathe the Eagles' slick and immaculately kept planes. Nothing is uglier to a Wolf than a brand-new-looking piece of hardware. The Wolves take great pride in showing off the superficial damages to their vehicles. They see them as great reminder of another good battle.

Pages 78–79
Chima Quiz

1. – C; 2. – B; 3. – A; 4. – B; 5. – C;
6. – A; 7. – A; 8. – B; 9. – C; 10. – B.